I SPY
TREASURE HUNT

A BOOK OF
PICTURE
RIDDLES

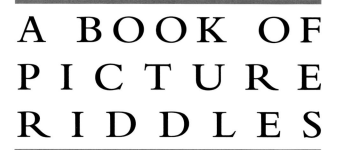

Photographs by Walter Wick

Riddles by Jean Marzollo

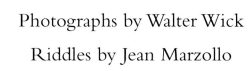

Cartwheel
·B·O·O·K·S·®

SCHOLASTIC INC.
New York   Toronto   London   Auckland   Sydney
Mexico City   New Delhi   Hong Kong   Buenos Aires

For Furlow, Chadwick, and Richard Word

W.W.

For Jennifer and Michelle Cotennec

J.M.

Book design by Carol Devine Carson

Go to www.scholastic.com for Web site information
on Scholastic authors and illustrators.

Library of Congress Cataloging-in-Publication Data

Wick, Walter.
    I spy treasure hunt: a book of picture riddles / photographs by Walter Wick; riddles by
Jean Marzollo.
        p.   cm.
    Summary: Rhyming verses ask readers to find hidden objects in the photographs.
    ISBN 0-439-04244-5
    1. Picture puzzles—Juvenile literature.   [1. Picture puzzles.]   I. Marzollo, Jean.   II. Title.
GV1507.P47W5296   1999
793.73—dc21   99-30581
                                                                                                   CIP
                            ISBN–13: 978-0-439-02674-1
                            ISBN–10: 0-439-02674-1
10 9 8 7 6 5 4 3 2 1   7 8 9 10 11/0

                        Printed in the Singapore
                This edition first printing, May 2007

TABLE OF CONTENTS

Picture riddles fill this book;
Turn the pages! Take a look!

Use your mind, use your eye;
Read the riddles—play I SPY!

I spy a sea horse, a thumbtack, a cone,

Scissors, a dolphin, a spoon, TELEPHONE;

A penny, a dog, and a rolling pin,
A hanger, a hatchet, and DUCK POND INN.

Standing on the porch of Duck Pond Inn,
I spy two coins, and a lazy clothespin;

Three dogs, two fishhooks, a broken oar,
A needle, a spool, and the TREASURE CHEST store.

I spy a dime, two dolphins, a tub,
Ten bowling pins, and a little golf club;

Two fishing poles, a leaning mousetrap,
A snowflake, a crab, two bats, and a map.

I spy three anchors, a small cannonball,

Five horses, a noose, and the word WATERFALL;

A shovel, a shark, two ships at port,
A bell, a boot, a mermaid, and FORT.

Standing in the fort and looking at the view,
I spy three ducks, a paintbrush, too;

A tortoise, a hare, a tea bag, a key,
A clock, and a flag on a house in a tree.

I spy a horseshoe, a hammer, a ski,
A lunch box, an owl, an upside-down tee;

A squirrel, two deer, five pinecones, a mouse,
A snake, a rake, and a distant lighthouse.

I spy a fishhook, an old paper clip,

A goose, a crab, and a cloudy ship;

A fish, a nail, a pencil, an oar,
The face of a man, and an X on a door.

21

I spy an oilcan, two loose screws,

Two saw blades, and seven horseshoes;

An eggshell, a nutshell, a seashell, and SOAP,
An old envelope, and a knot in a rope.

I spy a bird's nest, three spiders, a key,

A pulley, a pirate, and THINK OF ME;

A lady, a plate, an acorn cap,
Three snail shells, and another treasure map!

I spy a boot, a ruler, five jacks,
A hook, a saw, three starfish, an ax;

A skull and crossbones, a castle door,
And I'll get binoculars from page 24.

I spy a button, a walnut hull,

A bobby pin, the teeth of a skull;

A wishbone tree, a moon, a bell—
Are the teeth of the skull the stones of a well?

Hauling up treasure, I spy a note,

A camel, a leopard, a beetle, a boat;

An acorn, two lizards, a lock, and a key,
Three thimbles, three fish, five hearts: all for me!

EXTRA CREDIT RIDDLES

"Find Me" Riddle

I sit, I perch, I fly to and fro;

I'm in every picture; I'm a sleek black _____.

Find the Pictures That Go With These Riddles:

I spy a cat, a horse, and a lock,

A trapdoor, a nest, a reel, and a clock.

I spy a frog, five cats, five bees,

Four white hats, and four palm trees.

I spy a doghouse, a triangle stamp,

A birthday candle, and Aladdin's lamp.

I spy a sword, a shovel, a sail,

A dolphin, a hammer, a bottle, and WHALE.

I spy a key ring, a baseball, a horn,

A zipper pull tab, a fork, and corn.

I spy a lion, a spring, an oar,

A lobster claw, and a dinosaur.

I spy a tortoise, a teapot, a sword,

A dolphin, a shell, and a man overboard.

I spy a frog, a crown for a king,

A lantern, an owl, and a golden ring.

I spy a duck, a ruler, a broom,

A paddle, a cane, and a little mushroom.

I spy a poodle, a little red pail,

Five anchors, a cat, a duck, and a whale.

I spy a lizard, five bottles, a lock,

Shark teeth, an egg, and a fossil rock.

I spy an arrowhead, two turtles, a dog,

Antlers, a pinecone, a feather, and a frog.

How *I Spy Treasure Hunt* Was Made

I Spy Treasure Hunt is the tenth book in the I Spy series. For this book, I decided to do something different. Rather than build one set for each photograph as I did for previous I Spy books, I built a miniature village, a place called Smuggler's Cove, and photographed it from five points of view. To do this, I needed the help of an assistant and three freelance model-makers. Smuggler's Cove was built on a sixteen-by-sixteen-foot stage in HO scale (1:87). "The Treasure Chest Store," "The Map," "The Tree House and the Waterfall," "Shelter from the Storm," "The Cave," and "Treasure at Last!" were separate sets constructed at larger scales. "The Beach" was a large scale model used in combination with the HO scale landscape. All sets were photographed with a four-by-five-view camera. The entire project, from the planning and the sketches to the completion of the sets and photographs, took nine months. All the sets were taken apart. But they live on in the photographs, in the poetry of Jean Marzollo, and in the adventure we call *I Spy Treasure Hunt*.

I would like to thank the following people for helping me build the *I Spy Treasure Hunt* sets: Daniel Helt, for his assistance with the photography and model-making throughout the entire project; Bruce Morozko for his help with model-making and set construction on "The Tree House and the Waterfall," "The Cave," "The Beach," "Shelter from the Storm," "Treasure at Last!" and background details in "Arrival" and "View from the Fort"; Michael Lokensgard for fine detail work in "Arrival," "View from Duck Pond Inn," "View from the Fort," and "Shelter from the Storm"; John Bassano for assembling and painting many of the houses and other kit models used in the village; and Linda Cheverton-Wick for artistic advice, encouragement, and support on every aspect of the project. A special thanks to Scholastic editors Grace Maccarone and Bernette Ford, and to art director Edie Weinberg for their wise advice and kind patience. Also thanks to Will Altman, Barbara Ardizone, the Goff Family, Jeff Hirsch of Foto Care Limited NYC, and Rick Schwab of Rick's Image Works NYC.

Walter Wick

How to Write I Spy Riddles

The I Spy books help children look at the world more carefully, use language more vividly, and think more creatively. When I visit schools, I find that many students make wonderful I Spy pictures and that they often need help with their riddles. Here's some advice: (1) Look for interesting words, such as *thumbtack* and *hatchet*. (2) Put words like *shovel* and *shark* together because they have the same initial sound; that's called alliteration. (3) Put words like *crab*, *bats*, and *map* together because they have the same interior sound. Look for rhymes: oar/store, key/tree, jacks/ax. Rhythm and rhyme are essential! Every I Spy line has four measures, and each measure has three beats. To test your riddles, you can sing them to an old-fashioned song, "Sweet Betsy from Pike." If you learn it, you can sing your way through I Spy!

I would like to thank the following people for helping me test this book: the kids at Riverview Elementary School in Denville, NJ, and at Martin Elementary School in Manchester, CT; Michelle, Jennifer, and Donna Cotennec; Lura, Timothy, Julia, and Jonathan Briggs; Zak Colangelo and Ben Levine; Clea Colangelo and Stefan Jimenez; Allison Thompson, Katie Brennan, and Sri Kuehnlenz; Michaela, Stephen, and Kathy Everett; Mim Galligan, Sheila Rauch, and Margaret Hare; Chris and Molly Nowak, Claudio Marzollo, and once again Dave Marzollo for his outstanding creative output.

Jean Marzollo

About the Creators of *I Spy*

Jean Marzollo has written many award-winning children's books, including thirteen I Spy picture riddle books and seven I Spy Little books. She has also written: *I Love You: A Rebus Poem*, illustrated by Suse MacDonald; *I Am Planet Earth*, illustrated by Judith Moffatt; *Happy Birthday, Martin Luther King*, illustrated by Brian Pinkney; *Shanna's Princess Show* and *Shanna's Doctor Show*, illustrated by Shane Evans; *Pretend You're a Cat*, illustrated by Jerry Pinkney; *Mama Mama*, illustrated by Laura Regan; *Home Sweet Home*, illustrated by Ashley Wolff; *Soccer Sam*, illustrated by Blanche Sims; and *Close Your Eyes*, illustrated by Susan Jeffers. Most recently she has written and illustrated a highly acclaimed series of Bible stories for young children. For nineteen years, Jean Marzollo and Carol Carson produced Scholastic's kindergarten magazine, *Let's Find Out*. Ms. Marzollo holds a master's degree from the Harvard Graduate School of Education. She is the 2000 recipient of the Rip Van Winkle Award presented by the School Library Media Specialists of Southeastern New York. She lives with her husband, Claudio, in New York State's Hudson Valley.

Walter Wick is the photographer of the I Spy books. He is the author and photographer of *A Drop of Water: A Book of Science and Wonder*, which won the Boston Globe/Horn Book Award for Nonfiction, was named a Notable Children's Book by the American Library Association, and was selected as an Orbis Pictus Honor Book and a CBC/NSTA Outstanding Science Trade Book for Children. *Walter Wick's Optical Tricks*, a book of photographic illusions, was named a Best Illustrated Children's Book by the *New York Times Book Review*, was recognized as a Notable Children's Book by the American Library Association, and received many awards, including the Platinum Award from the Oppenheim Toy Portfolio, a Young Reader's Award from *Scientific American*, a *Bulletin* Blue Ribbon, and a Parent's Choice Silver Honor. His most recent series, Can You See What I See?, has appeared on the *New York Times* Bestseller List. Mr. Wick has invented photographic games for *Games* magazine and photographed covers for books and magazines, including *Newsweek*, *Discover*, and *Psychology Today*. A graduate of Paier College of Art, Mr. Wick lives with his wife, Linda, in Connecticut.

Carol Devine Carson, the book designer for the I Spy series, is art director for a major publishing house in New York City.

I Spy Books for All Ages:
I SPY: A BOOK OF PICTURE RIDDLES
I SPY CHRISTMAS
I SPY EXTREME CHALLENGER!
I SPY FANTASY
I SPY FUN HOUSE
I SPY GOLD CHALLENGER!
I SPY MYSTERY
I SPY SCHOOL DAYS
I SPY SPOOKY NIGHT
I SPY SUPER CHALLENGER!
I SPY TREASURE HUNT
I SPY ULTIMATE CHALLENGER
I SPY YEAR-ROUND CHALLENGER!

Books for New Readers:
SCHOLASTIC READER LVL 1: I SPY A BALLOON
SCHOLASTIC READER LVL 1: I SPY A BUTTERFLY
SCHOLASTIC READER LVL 1: I SPY A CANDY CANE
SCHOLASTIC READER LVL 1: I SPY A DINOSAUR'S EYE
SCHOLASTIC READER LVL 1: I SPY A PENGUIN
SCHOLASTIC READER LVL 1: I SPY A PUMPKIN
SCHOLASTIC READER LVL 1: I SPY A SCARY MONSTER
SCHOLASTIC READER LVL 1: I SPY A SCHOOL BUS
SCHOLASTIC READER LVL 1: I SPY FUNNY TEETH
SCHOLASTIC READER LVL 1: I SPY LIGHTNING IN THE SKY
SCHOLASTIC READER LVL 1: I SPY SANTA CLAUS

And for the Youngest Child:
I SPY LITTLE ANIMALS
I SPY LITTLE BOOK
I SPY LITTLE BUNNIES
I SPY LITTLE CHRISTMAS
I SPY LITTLE LEARNING BOX
I SPY LITTLE LETTERS
I SPY LITTLE NUMBERS
I SPY LITTLE WHEELS

Also Available:
I SPY CHALLENGER FOR GAME BOY ADVANCE
I SPY JUNIOR: PUPPET PLAYHOUSE CD-ROM
I SPY JUNIOR CD-ROM
I SPY SCHOOL DAYS CD-ROM
I SPY SPOOKY MANSION CD-ROM
I SPY TREASURE HUNT CD-ROM